This Book Belongs

to

Laurie Roy

from

Lois and Zane

Christmas, 1959

Shirley Temple's Fairyland

Shirley Temple's
Fairyland

The Wild Swans
Beauty and the Beast
Rumpelstiltskin
The Sleeping Beauty

RANDOM HOUSE · NEW YORK

The Wild Swans

The Wild Swans

ILLUSTRATED BY TOM O'SULLIVAN

FAR AWAY, in a land where the swallows fly when our winter comes, there once lived a King who had eleven sons and one daughter. The eleven brothers—the young Princes—went to school each with a star on his breast and a sword at his side. They wrote upon slates of gold with pencils of diamond, and learned to say their lessons by heart as if they were reading them from a book; one could see that they were Princes. Their sister Elise sat upon a little glass stool, and had a picture-book which cost half a kingdom. Oh, these children had a happy time, but it was not to remain so.

Their father, who was King of the whole country, married a wicked Queen who did not love his poor children at all. On the very first day they knew this. In the Palace there was great feasting; but the children, instead of getting all the cakes and roasted apples they could eat, as they used to do, were only given some sand in a teacup, and told they might pretend it was something good.

The next week, the Queen took little Elise into the country to a peasant and his wife; and it was not long before the wicked Queen had told the King so many falsehoods about the poor Princes that he did not trouble himself about them any more.

"Fly out into the world and get your own living," the wicked Queen told the Princes. "Fly like great birds without a voice." But she could not do all the harm she had intended, for the Princes turned into eleven beautiful white swans. With a strange cry they flew out of the Palace windows, far over the park and into the wood.

It was still quite early morning when they came by the place where their sister Elise lay asleep in the peasant's house. Here they hovered over the roof, turned their long necks, and flapped their wings, but no one heard or saw them. They had to fly on, high up towards the clouds, far away into the wide world, and into a great dark wood which stretched away to the seashore.

Poor little Elise was standing in the peasant's house playing with a green leaf, for she had no other playthings. She picked a hole in the leaf, and looked through it up at the sun, and it seemed to her that she saw her brothers' clear eyes. When the warm sun shone on her cheeks, she remembered their kisses.

Each day passed just like the rest. When the wind swept through the rose bushes outside the house, it whispered to the roses, "Could anyone be more beautiful than you?" Then the roses answered, "Yes, Elise!" And on Sundays, when the old peasant woman sat in front of her door, reading her hymnbook, the wind turned the pages and said to the book, "Who can be more pious than you?" "Elise!" said the hymnbook: and what the roses and the hymnbook said was the simple truth.

When she was fifteen years old Elise was to go home. But when the Queen saw how beautiful she was, she was filled with hatred towards her. She would gladly have turned her into a wild swan like her brothers, but she did not dare to do so at once, for the King wished to see his daughter.

Early the next morning the Queen went into the great bathroom, which was built of white marble and decked with soft cushions and beautiful rugs. She took three toads, kissed them, and said to the first, "Sit upon Elise's head when she comes into the bath, so

that she may become as stupid as you! Sit upon her forehead," she said to the second, "so that she may become as ugly as you, and that her father may not know her. Rest upon her heart," she whispered to the third, "so that she may now have an evil mind and suffer from it."

Then the Queen put the toads into the clear water, which at once turned a green color. Calling Elise, she bade her undress and go into the water. As Elise plunged in, the first toad sat upon her hair, the second on her forehead, and the third on her heart, but she did not seem to notice it. When she rose, three red poppies were seen floating on the water. If the creatures had not been poisonous, and had not been kissed by the witch, they would have been changed into red roses; yet they became flowers because they had rested on Elise's head and heart. She was too good and too innocent for witchcraft to have power over her.

When the wicked Queen saw that, she rubbed Elise with walnut juice so that she became dark brown, smeared a harmful ointment on her face and let her beautiful hair hang in a tangle. No one would have recognized her.

When her father saw her, he was shocked, and declared this was not his daughter. No one recognized her but the dog and the swallows, but they were poor animals who could say nothing.

Then poor Elise wept and thought of her eleven brothers who had disappeared. Sadly she stole out of the castle. She wandered all day over field and moor as far as the great wood. She did not know where to go; but felt very sorrowful, and longed for her brothers; they had probably been, like herself, driven out into the wide world, and she must find them. She had been only a short time in the wood when night fell. She had lost the path, so she lay down upon the soft moss, said her evening prayer and rested her head against the stump of a tree.

The whole night she dreamed of her brothers. They were children again playing together, writing with their diamond pencils upon their golden slates. Only they were not writing lines and letters, as they used to do, but writing of all they had seen and experienced.

When Elise awoke, the sun was already high. She could not see it, for the lofty trees spread their branches above her, but the rays played above like a gauzy veil. She heard the splashing of water from a number of springs all flowing into a lake with the most delightful sandy bottom. It was surrounded by thick bushes, but in one place the deer had trampled a large opening and here Elise could get to the water. It was so clear that every leaf was clearly mirrored on the smooth water.

When Elise saw her own face, she was frightened; it was so brown and ugly; but when she wetted her little hand and rubbed her eyes and forehead, the white skin appeared again. Then she undressed and went down into the fresh water, and a more beautiful King's daughter could not have been found in all the world.

When she had dressed herself again and plaited her long hair, she went to the bubbling spring and drank from the hollow of her hand. Then she wandered deeper into the wood, not knowing where she went. She thought of her brothers, and she knew that Heaven would not forsake her. God had made the wild apples grow to feed the hungry, and He showed her a tree with the boughs bending under the weight of its fruit. Here she took her midday meal and, having propped up the heavy boughs, went into the darkest part of the forest. It was so quiet there that she could hear her own footsteps. Here was such a solitude as she had never before known.

The night came on very dark; not a single glowworm now gleamed in the grass. Sorrowfully Elise lay down to sleep. Then it seemed to her as if the branches above her parted, and the sweet eyes of angels looked down upon her. When morning came she did not know if she had dreamed it, or if it had really been true.

She walked a few steps forward. Then she met an old woman with a basket full of berries. The woman gave her a few of them, and Elise asked her if she had not seen eleven Princes riding through the wood.

"No," replied the old woman, "but yesterday I saw eleven swans, with golden crowns on their heads, swimming down the stream close by."

She led Elise a little further on, to where a little river wound its way. The trees on either side stretched their long leafy branches toward each other. Elise said good-by to the old woman, and followed the river to the place where it flowed out to the open ocean.

The whole glorious sea lay before the young Princess' eyes, but not a sail appeared, not a single boat was to be seen. How was she to go on? She looked at the countless little pebbles on the shore which the water had worn quite smooth. Glass, iron, stones, all that had been washed up had been rounded by the water which was even softer than Elise's delicate hands.

"It rolls on unweariedly, and thus what is hard becomes smooth. I will be just as unwearied! Thanks for your lesson, you clear rolling waves! My heart tells me that one day you will lead me to my dear brothers."

On the sea-grass lay eleven white swan's feathers, which she collected. Drops of water were on them—whether they were dewdrops or tears she could not tell. It was very lonely there, but she did not mind it, for the sea was ever changing.

When the sun was just about to set, Elise saw eleven wild swans, with golden crowns on their heads, flying toward the land; they swept along, one behind the other, so that they looked like a long white band. She climbed down the slope and hid herself behind a bush. The swans alighted near her and flapped their great white wings.

As soon as the sun had disappeared beneath the water, the swans' feathers fell off, and there stood eleven handsome Princes, Elise's brothers. She uttered a loud cry, for although they were greatly altered, she knew them. She sprang into their arms, and called them by their names. The Princes were overjoyed when they saw their little sister again; they knew her, too, though she was now tall and beautiful. They laughed and wept, and soon understood how cruel their stepmother had been to them all.

"We brothers," said the eldest, "fly about as wild swans as long

as the sun is in the sky, but when it has set we return to our human form. Therefore at sunset we must take care to have ground under our feet, for if we were then flying up among the clouds, we would sink into the sea as men. We do not live here. A land just as fair as this lies beyond this sea. But it is far and we must cross the mighty ocean to reach it, and on the way there is no island where we could pass the night. But one single little rock rises from the waves; it is just large enough for us to rest upon it close to one another. If the sea is rough, the foam spurts over us, yet we thank God for the rock. There we pass the night in our human form; were it not for this rock, we could never visit our beloved native land, for the journey requires two of the longest days in the year. Only once each year can we visit our home, and then we dare stay only eleven days. When we fly over the great wood we can see the Palace in which we were born and in which our father lives, and the high church tower where our mother lies buried. Here is our own land, to which we feel ourselves drawn—and here we have found you, our dear little sister. Two more days we may stay here; then we must fly over the sea to a land that is beautiful but is not our native land. How can we bear you away? We have neither ship nor boat."

"How can I release you?" asked the sister.

They went on talking far into the night, sleeping only for a few hours. Elise was awakened by the sound of swans' wings above her. Her brothers were again transformed and flew in wide circles, and, at last, far away. But one of them, the youngest, stayed behind, and the swan laid his head in her lap, and she stroked his wings. They remained together the whole day. Towards evening the others came back, and when the sun had gone down they stood there in their human form.

"Tomorrow we fly far away," they told Elise, "and cannot come back for a whole year. But we cannot leave you like this! Have you the courage to come with us? Should not all our wings be strong enough to carry you over the sea?"

"Yes, take me with you!" cried Elise.

That whole night they wove a net of willow bark and tough reeds, and it was great and strong. Elise lay down on this net, and when the sun rose and her brothers were changed into wild swans, they seized the net with their beaks, and flew with their beloved sister who was still asleep high up toward the clouds. The sunbeams fell upon her face, and one of the swans flew over her head to shade her with his broad wings.

They were far from land when Elise awoke. She thought she was still dreaming, for it seemed so strange to be carried through the air, high over the sea. By her side lay a branch with beautiful ripe berries, and a bundle of sweet-tasting roots. The youngest brother had gathered them and placed them there for her. She smiled at him thankfully, for she recognized him; it was he who flew over her and shaded her with his wings.

The whole day they flew on through the air, but their flight was slower than usual, for they had their sister to carry. Bad weather came on. As evening drew near, Elise looked anxiously at the setting sun for the lonely rock in the ocean could not be seen. It seemed to her that the swans beat the air more strongly with their wings. Alas! it was her fault that they could not fly fast enough; at sunset they must become men and fall into the sea and drown. She prayed from the depths of her heart. Dark clouds rolled near; and the lightning burst forth, flash after flash.

Now the sun touched the edge of the sea. Elise's heart trembled. Then suddenly the swans darted downward so swiftly that she thought they were falling. The sun was half hidden below the water. And now for the first time Elise saw the little rock beneath her. It looked no larger than a seal thrusting its head out of the water. The sun sank very fast; at last it seemed only like a star and then Elise's foot touched the rock. The sun went out like the last spark in a burned paper. Her brothers were standing around her, arm in arm—but there was only just room enough for them and her. The sea beat against the rock and over her like small rain, the sky glowing with continual fire while the thunder rolled. Sister and brothers held one another by the hand and sang a psalm, which gave them comfort and courage.

At dawn the air was pure and calm. As soon as the sun rose, the swans flew away from the island with Elise. When the sun rose higher, Elise saw before her, half floating in the air, a mountainous country with shining masses of ice on the water. In the midst of it rose a castle with row above row of columns. Palm trees swayed below, and there were flowers as large as millwheels. Elise asked if this was the land to which they were bound, but the swans shook their heads, for what she beheld was the gorgeous ever-changing palace of Fata Morgana into which they might bring no human being. As Elise gazed at it, mountain, woods, and castle suddenly crumbled, and in their place stood twenty proud churches, all nearly alike, with high towers and pointed windows. She fancied she heard the sound of organs, but it was the sea she heard. When she was quite near the churches they seemed to change into a fleet of ships sailing beneath her, but when she looked down it was only the sea mist over the ocean. A continual change kept passing before her eyes, till at last she made out the real land to which they were bound. There arose the most glorious blue mountains with cedar forests, cities, and palaces. Long before the sun went down, Elise was sitting on a rock in front of a great cave overgrown with green trailing plants that looked like embroidered carpets.

"Now we shall see what you will dream of here tonight," said the youngest brother, and he showed her where she was to sleep.

"I hope that I may dream of a way to set you free," she replied. This thought possessed her, and she prayed ardently for help; even in her sleep she continued to pray. Then it seemed to her as if she were flying high in the air to the cloudy palace of Fata Morgana; and a fairy came out to meet her, beautiful and radiant. And yet the fairy looked quite like the old woman who had given her the berries in the wood and had told her of the swans with golden crowns on their heads.

"Your brothers can be set free," she said, "but have you courage and perseverance? Water is softer than your delicate hands, and yet it changes the shape of stones, but it does not feel the pain your fingers will feel; it has no heart, and cannot suffer the agony and torment you will have to endure. Do you see the stinging nettle I hold in my hand? This kind grows plentifully around the cave in which you sleep. Those only and those that grow on the graves in the churchyard must be used—remember that! Those you must pluck, though they will burn your hands into blisters. Break these nettles with your feet, and you will have flax. Of this you must plait and weave eleven shirts of mail with long sleeves; throw these over the eleven swans, and the charm will be broken. But listen well: from the moment you begin this work until it is finished, even though it should take years, you must not speak! The first word you utter will pierce your brothers' hearts like a deadly dagger. Their lives hang on your tongue. Remember!"

She touched Elise's hand with the nettles; it was like a burning fire, and Elise woke with the smart. It was broad daylight; and close by the spot where she had slept lay a nettle like the one she had seen in her dream. She fell on her knees and prayed gratefully, and went out from the cave to begin her work.

With her delicate hands she groped among the ugly nettles. They stung like fire, burning great blisters on her arms and hands; but she thought she could bear it gladly if she could only free her dear brothers. Then she crushed every nettle with her bare feet and plaited the green flax.

When the sun had set, her brothers came, and they were frightened when they found her dumb. They thought it was some new sorcery of their wicked stepmother's; but when they saw her hands they understood what she was doing for their sake. The youngest brother wept, and where his tears dropped Elise felt no pain, and the burning blisters vanished.

She worked the whole night, for she could not sleep until she had freed her dear brothers. All the following day, while the swans were away, she sat in solitude, but never had time flown so quickly. One shirt was already finished and now she began the second.

Then a hunting horn sounded in the hills and she was struck with fear. As the noise came nearer, and she heard the barking dogs, she fled into the cave. There she bound into a bundle the nettles she had gathered, and sat upon the bundle.

A big hound came bounding out of the ravine, and then another, and another. They barked loudly, ran back, and then came on again. In a few minutes all the huntsmen stood outside the cave. The handsomest of them was the King of the country. He came forward to Elise, for he had never seen a more beautiful maiden.

"How did you come here, you delightful child?" he asked.

Elise shook her head, for she might not speak—it would cost her brothers their deliverance and their lives. She hid her hands under her apron so that the King might not see what she was suffering.

"Come with me," he said. "You cannot stay here. If you are as good as you are beautiful, I will dress you in velvets and silks and place the golden crown on your head, and you shall dwell in my richest castle and rule."

Then he lifted her onto his horse. Elise wept and wrung her hands, but the King said, "I only wish your happiness; one day you will thank me for this." And placing her behind him on his horse, he galloped away among the mountains, while the huntsmen followed after them.

At sunset the fair regal city, with its churches and cupolas, lay before them. The King led Elise into the castle where great fountains played in the lofty marble halls. The walls and ceilings were covered with glorious pictures. But the poor young Princess had no eyes for all this. She only wept and grieved. Passively she let the women dress her in royal robes, and weave pearls in her hair, and draw soft gloves over her blistered fingers.

When she was fully arrayed, she was so dazzlingly beautiful that the court bowed deeper than before. The King chose her for his bride. But now the King's advisor shook his head and whispered that the beautiful maid was certainly a witch, who blinded the eyes and led astray the King's heart.

The King gave no heed to this. He ordered that music should

sound, and the costliest dishes be served, and that the most beautiful maidens should dance before him and his betrothed. Elise was led through fragrant gardens into gorgeous halls; but never a smile came to her lips or shone in her eyes. There she stood, a picture of grief. Then the King opened the door to a little chamber close by, where she was to sleep. It was decked with green tapestry, to resemble the cave in which the King had found her. On the floor lay the bundle of flax she had prepared from the nettles, and from the ceiling hung the shirt of mail she had completed. One of the huntsmen had brought these things with him as curiosities.

"Here you may dream yourself back in your former home," said the King. "Here is the work you were doing there. Now, in the midst of all your splendor, it will amuse you to think of that time."

When Elise saw these things that were so dear to her heart, a smile played around her mouth, and the blood came back into her cheeks. She thought of her brothers' deliverance, and kissed the King's hand. He pressed her to his heart, and ordered all the church bells to announce the marriage feast. The beautiful dumb girl out of the wood was to be Queen of the country!

Then the King's advisor again whispered evil words in the King's ear, but again they did not sink into the King's heart. The marriage would take place. The King's advisor himself was obliged to place the crown on Elise's head, and with wicked spite he pressed the narrow circlet so tightly upon her brow that it hurt her. But a heavier ring lay around her heart; sorrow for her brothers. She remained dumb, for a single word would have cost her brothers their lives. But her eyes glowed with love for the kind, handsome King who did everything to please her. She loved him with her whole heart, more and more every day. Oh, if she could only confide in him of her grief! But she must remain dumb and finish her work in silence. Therefore at night she stole away from his side and went quietly to the little chamber that was decorated like the cave, and wove one shirt of mail after another. But when she began the seventh she had no flax left to finish it.

She knew that the nettles she could use were growing in the churchyard, but she must pluck them herself, and how was she to go out there?

"Oh, what is the pain in my fingers compared with the torment my heart endures!" she thought. "I must venture it, and help will not be denied me!" With a trembling heart, as though she were doing something evil, she crept into the garden one moonlight night and through the lanes and the deserted streets to the churchyard. There she saw a circle af lamias sitting on one of the broadest tomb-stones. These hideous wretches took off their rags as if they were going to bathe; then with their skinny fingers they clawed open the fresh graves. Elise had to pass close by them, and they fastened their evil eyes upon her, but she prayed silently and gathered the burning nettles, and carried them back to the castle.

Only one person had seen her and that was the King's advisor. He was awake while the others slept. Now he felt sure that all was not

as it should be with the Queen. She was a witch and she had bewitched the King and the whole people.

In secret, he told the King what he had seen and what he feared, and as he spoke these hard words, the pictures of saints in the cathedral shook their heads, as though they said: "It is not true, Elise is innocent." But the King's advisor chose to interpret this differently; he said they were bearing witness against her, and shaking their heads at her sinfulness. Then two heavy tears rolled down the King's cheeks; he went home with doubt in his heart. At night he pretended to be asleep, but no peace came to him for he noticed that Elise got up every night. Each time he followed her silently and saw how she disappeared from her chamber.

Now she had almost finished her work; only one shirt of mail remained to be completed, but she had no flax left and not a single nettle. Once more, for the last time, she must go to the churchyard to pluck a few handfuls of nettles. She thought with terror of the horrible lamias, but her will was as firm as her trust in Providence.

Elise went, but the King and his advisor followed her. They saw her vanish through the gate into the churchyard, and when they drew near, the lamias were sitting on the tombstone as Elise had seen them. The King turned away, for he imagined she was amongst them—she whose head had rested against his breast that very evening.

"The people must judge her," he said. And the people condemned her to suffer death by fire.

Out of the regal halls she was led into a dark damp cell, where the wind whistled through the barred window. Instead of silk and velvet she was given the bundle of nettles she had gathered. She was to lay her head upon this, and the hard burning coats of mail were to be her coverlet. But she was not dismayed; indeed, she could not have been given anything that would have pleased her more. She started her work again, and prayed. Outside, the boys on the street were singing jeering songs about her, and not a soul comforted her with a kind word.

But toward evening there came the whirring of a swan's wings close to the grating; it was the youngest of her brothers. Elise sobbed aloud for joy, though she knew that the coming night might be the last she had to live; however, her work was almost done, and her brothers were here.

Now the King's advisor came to stay with her in her last hour, for he had promised the King to do so. But Elise shook her head, and with looks and gestures begged him to leave her. For in this night she must finish her work, or all would have been in vain—all her suffering, and all her tears. The King's advisor withdrew, uttering evil words against her; but poor Elise knew she was innocent, and went on with her work.

It was still an hour before sunrise when the eleven brothers stood at the castle gate and demanded to be brought before the King. This could not be done, they were told, for the King was asleep and might not be disturbed. They begged and they threatened and the sentries turned out, and even the King himself came out and asked what the disturbance meant. At that moment the sun rose and the brothers were no more to be seen, but eleven wild swans were seen flying away over the castle.

All the people came streaming out at the town gate to see the witch burned. An old horse drew the cart on which Elise sat. She had been clothed in a garment of coarse sackcloth; her lovely hair hung loose about her beautiful head; her cheeks were pale as death, and her lips moved silently while her fingers busied themselves with the green flax. Even on the way to her death she did not interrupt the work she had begun. The ten shirts of mail lay at her feet and she was working on the eleventh.

The mob jeered, "Look at the witch, how she mutters! She has no hymn-book in her hand, no—it's her ugly sorcery, that's what she's holding. Tear it in a thousand pieces!"

They all pressed upon her to tear up the shirts of mail. Suddenly eleven white swans swept down, sat round about her on the cart, and beat with their great wings. The mob fell back before them, terrified.

"That is a sign from heaven! She is innocent!" many whispered.

But they did not dare to say it aloud.

Now the executioner seized Elise by the hand, but she hastily threw the eleven shirts over the swans, and in a twinkling eleven handsome Princes stood there. But the youngest had a swan's wing instead of an arm, for Elise had not quite finished the second sleeve of his shirt.

"Now I may speak!" she said. "I am innocent."

And the people who saw what had happened bowed before her as before a saint. But she sank as if lifeless into the arms of her brothers. The suspense, the anguish, and the pain had exhausted her.

"Yes, she is innocent," said the eldest brother, and he told them all that had happened. While he spoke, a fragrance arose of millions of roses, for every fagot at the stake had taken root and put forth branches, and a great fragrant hedge appeared covered with red roses. At the top was a single white flower, shining and gleaming like a star. The King picked this flower and laid it on Elise's bosom, and she arose with peace and happiness in her heart.

And all the church bells rang out of their own accord, and birds came in great flocks. And back to the castle went a magnificent procession.

Beauty and the Beast

Beauty and the Beast

ILLUSTRATED BY PAUL BACON

ONCE UPON A TIME, in a very far-off country, there lived a merchant who had been so fortunate in all his undertakings that he was enormously rich. His ships sailed the seas bringing treasures from the far corners of the earth. He and his three daughters lived in great luxury in a fine house in the town.

But suddenly misfortune befell them. The merchant lost every ship he had upon the sea, either through pirates, shipwreck, or fire. Then he found that his clerks in distant countries, whom he trusted, had cheated him; and at last from great wealth he fell into the direst poverty.

All he had left was a little cottage in a desolate place in the forest, and to this he was forced to retreat with his daughters, who were in despair at the idea of leading such a different life. Now they found that they were left alone, and that their former friends who had been so numerous while they were rich, showed no intention of offering them any help.

As they were now too poor to have servants, the girls had to work hard. They complained constantly at having to live without the luxuries and amusements of their former life; only the youngest one tried to be brave and cheerful. She had been as sad as anyone when misfortune first overtook her father, but she soon set to work to make the best of things. She tried to amuse her father and to persuade her sisters to join her in dancing and singing. Because she was so cheerful, they declared that this miserable life was all she was fit for. She was really far prettier and cleverer than they; indeed, she was so lovely to look at that she was always called Beauty.

After two years, when they were all beginning to get used to their new life, the merchant received news that one of his ships, which he had believed lost, had come safely into port with a rich cargo. The daughters, thinking that now they would be rich again, wanted to set out directly for the town. But their father, who was more prudent, begged them to wait a little; he would go by himself to make inquiries.

So they loaded their father with requests that he bring them jewels and dresses which it would have taken a fortune to buy. Only Beauty did not ask for anything. Her father said: "And what shall I bring for you, Beauty?"

"The only thing I wish is for you to come home safely," she answered.

But her father thought there must be some pretty thing she would want, so he begged her to name it.

"Well, dear father," she said, "as you insist upon it, I beg that you will bring me a rose. I have not seen one since we came here, and I love them so much."

The merchant set out and reached the town as quickly as possible, only to find that his ship had been seized and sold to pay his debts. So after months of trouble and expense he started back to the cottage poorer than ever. To make matters worse, it was mid-winter now and he was obliged to leave the town in the most terrible weather, so that by the time he was within a few leagues of his home he was almost exhausted with cold and fatigue. He was in the deep forest when night overtook him. The falling snow had covered up every trail, and he did not know which way to turn.

At length he made out some sort of path, and this led him into a lovely garden, at the end of which stood a splendid castle, its windows blazing with light. It seemed to the merchant very strange that no snow had fallen in the garden, which was in full bloom. He walked on in wonderment until he came to the great door of the castle. A golden horn hung on a chair beside it. After a moment's hesitation the merchant put the horn to his lips and blew it. At once the door opened, and he stepped into a wide and noble hall brilliantly lighted with golden lamps. He called aloud but there was no answer. There seemed to be nobody in all this vast and splendid palace. Going further into the great room he found a fire blazing on the hearth. A couch was drawn up cozily and before it a table had been set for one. Thinking that this must be prepared for someone who was expected, the merchant sat down to wait.

But he was terribly hungry and wished there were someone whom he could ask to give him something to eat. He glanced again at the litle table and saw that a delicious dinner had been placed on it. Now an unseen hand lifted the covers from the dishes, and the chair was moved back a little to receive him. "It seems," he thought, "this dinner is meant for me." As he had eaten nothing for twenty-four hours, he lost no time in beginning his meal, hoping that he might soon have an opportunity of thanking his considerate host, whoever it might be. But no one appeared. Now he noticed that the couch was made up into a bed. Taking off his boots and jacket, the merchant fell into the bed and was soon fast asleep. When he awoke completely refreshed, he saw that a complete outfit of handsome new clothes had replaced his worn ones. There was still no sign of anybody, even though a fresh meal of dainty cakes and fruit had been placed upon the little table at his elbow. After satisfying his appetite, he dressed and went down into the garden. And here, though it was winter everywhere else, the sun shone, the birds sang, flowers bloomed, and the air was soft and sweet. Along the path a hedge of beautiful roses reminded him of his promise to Beauty. He stopped and had just plucked one to take to her when he was startled by a strange noise

behind him. Turning around, he was faced by a frightful Beast, which seemed very angry and said in a terrible voice:

"Who told you that you might gather my roses? Was it not enough that I sheltered you in my palace and was kind to you? Is this the way you thank me, by robbing me of my roses? But your insolence shall not go unpunished."

The merchant, terrified by these furious words, dropped the rose and, throwing himself on his knees, cried: "Pardon me, noble sir. I am truly grateful to you for your hospitality, which was so magnificent that I could not imagine you would be offended by my taking such a little thing as a rose."

But the Beast was still angry. "You are very ready with excuses and flattery," he cried; "but that will not save you from the death you deserve."

"Alas!" thought the merchant. "If my daughter Beauty could only know what danger her rose has brought me into!"

And in despair he told the Beast of his misfortunes, and the reason of his journey, and especially of Beauty's request.

"A king's ransom would hardly have procured all that my other daughters asked," he said; "but I thought that I might at least take Beauty her rose. I beg you to forgive me, for you see I meant no harm."

The Beast thought for a moment, and then he said:

"I will spare you on one condition—that is, that you will give me one of your daughters."

"Ah!" cried the merchant. "Even if I were cruel enough to buy my own life at the cost of one of my children's what excuse could I invent to bring her here?"

"No excuse!" thundered the Beast. "She must come of her own free will if she loves you enough to want to save your life. On no other condition will I have her. Return in a month with one of your daughters if one of them is courageous enough to come back with you and stay here, in order to let you go free. Otherwise you must return alone. And do not imagine that you can hide from me," added the Beast grimly, "for if you do not return in a month I will come and fetch you!"

The merchant accepted this proposal, though he did not really intend to bring any of his daughters. He wanted only to go and see them for the last time.

"Now farewell," said the Beast. "Take a rose to Beauty and remember your promise!"

The merchant was only too glad when the Beast left him. He gathered up Beauty's rose, and went off swiftly to the cottage in the forest.

His daughters rushed to meet him, eager to know the result of

his journey. And when they saw him dressed in rich new clothes, they supposed he had good news. He hid the truth from them at first, only saying sadly to Beauty as he gave her the rose:

"Here is what you asked me to bring you. Little do you know how much it cost."

But this excited their curiosity so greatly that he had to tell his adventure from beginning to end. Now the two older girls were very angry with Beauty. If she had asked for something sensible, they said, this would never have happened. It was all her fault, they kept repeating.

Poor Beauty, much distressed, said to them:

"Who could have guessed that to ask for a rose would cause so much misery? But as I caused this mischief it is only just that I should go back with my father to keep his promise."

At first nobody would hear of this, and her father declared that he would never let her go. But Beauty was firm. And as the time drew near she divided her few possessions between her sisters, and said good-by to everything she loved. When the fatal day came she encouraged and cheered her father as they went together toward the path by which he had come. But still he begged her to reconsider. "The Beast would destroy you," he said. "We would never see you again."

But Beauty said: "Take courage, Father. He may not be so bad if he loves roses so much."

Her father shook his head sadly: "Do not delude yourself with hope, my child. The Beast is not only monstrous to look at—he is ferocious beyond words."

To this, Beauty replied: "Is it not possible, Father, for a beast to be tamed?"

When they had nearly reached the palace they saw that it was brilliantly lit from the roof to the ground. The garden was hung with lanterns, and soft music sounded from the courtyard.

"The Beast must be very hungry," said Beauty, trying to laugh, "if he makes all this rejoicing over the arrival of his prey."

But, in spite of her fears, she could not help admiring all the wonderful scene before her.

Again, as before, the great door of the palace opened by itself and closed after them. The merchant led Beauty into the room he had been in before. There they found a blazing fire, and the table daintily spread with a magnificent feast for two.

The merchant knew that this was meant for them. Beauty was too frightened to be hungry, but feared it would anger the Beast if they ignored his hospitality. They had barely finished their meal when the noise of the Beast's footsteps was heard approaching. Beauty clung to her father in terror. But when the Beast really appeared she made a great effort to hide her horror, and saluted him respectfully.

This evidently pleased the Beast. He looked at her in silence. Then he said:

"Good evening, old man. Good evening, Beauty."

The merchant was too terrified to reply, but Beauty answered sweetly:

"Good evening, sir."

"I am the Beast," he said. "You will call me that, please."

"Good evening, Beast," Beauty said, politely.

"Have you come willingly?" asked the Beast. "Will you be content to stay here when your father goes away?"

Beauty answered bravely that she was quite prepared to stay.

"I am pleased with you," said the Beast. "And as you have come of your own accord, you may stay. You will find everything in readiness for your comfort. If you find anything lacking you have only to speak your wish and it will be fulfilled." Then, turning to the merchant, he said: "Upon your return home you will find a sack filled with gold awaiting you. You may consider it a remembrance from Beauty to her sisters."

Then in a stern voice: "Now leave this palace, merchant. And do not expect ever to return to it." Then he went away, after saying, "Good-by, Beauty; good-by, old man."

Now the merchant clung to Beauty, weeping: "Oh, my child, I cannot leave you alone here. I fear I shall never see you again."

But Beauty comforted him: "We must not lose hope, Father. Go now. Go quickly, or my heart will break." Slowly her father moved toward the great door. It opened and then closed after him. Now Beauty was alone. She sank down on the couch and wept quietly.

Suddenly the silence in the room was broken by the sound of soft music. Beauty arose and walked toward the room from which the music seemed to be coming. At the door she paused. On it, in beautiful letters, were the words: "Beauty's Room." Greatly surprised, she entered and looked about in wonder. The room was filled with beautiful things; on the table lay heaps of dazzling jewels and in the closets were dresses fit for a queen. Everywhere were things for her comfort. Beauty went from treasure to treasure, looking at them in bewilderment. Finally her eyes rested on a small picture in a golden frame, hanging on the wall. It was a picture of a young prince, and Beauty thought she had never seen anyone so handsome.

Now she began to feel very sleepy, and lay down on the snowy bed that was prepared for her. She fell asleep at once. And as she slept, she had a dream. She dreamed that she was walking by a brook bordered with trees, when the handsome young prince of the picture came to her and said, "Ah, Beauty! You are not so unfortunate as you suppose. Here you will be rewarded for all you have suffered elsewhere. Your every wish shall be granted. Only try to find me out, no matter how I may be disguised. I am a prisoner here in the castle of the Beast. Find me, and set me free."

"Tell me how to find you, dear Prince," said Beauty.

"Find me with your heart," he answered, "and do not trust too much to your eyes. Above all, do not desert me until you have saved me from my cruel misery. Without you I shall die."

When Beauty awoke she found her dressing table set out with everything she could possibly want. When she had bathed and dressed she found a delicious breakfast awaiting her. She thought of her dream prince, and looked again at the picture to see if he was the same.

"He said that I should find him," said Beauty to herself. "It seems, then, that this horrible Beast keeps him a prisoner. How can I set him free? I wonder why he told me not to trust too much to my eyes? I don't understand it. But, then, it was only a dream."

To pass the time she began to explore some of the many rooms of the palace, half hoping to find the prince of her dream. The first she entered was lined with mirrors, and Beauty saw herself reflected on every side. Then a bracelet which was hanging from a chandelier caught her eye, and on taking it down she was greatly surprised to find that it held a portrait of her unknown prince, just as she had seen him in her dream. With great delight she slipped the bracelet on her arm. Then she passed through into a room which contained every musical instrument. The next room was a library, and it seemed to her that a whole lifetime would not be enough even to read the names of the books, there were so many. So the day passed and it was growing dusk; wax candles in diamond and ruby candlesticks were beginning to light themselves in every room. And still Beauty had not seen anyone nor heard a single voice.

She found her supper served just at the time she wished to have it. But she began to be rather lonely, and to wonder when she would see the Beast again.

Presently she heard him coming, and she could not help trembling. Perhaps he would be angry with her.

However, he did not seem at all ferocious, and only said gruffly: "Good evening, Beauty."

She answered cheerfully and managed to conceal her terror. Then the Beast asked if she had found everything to her liking, and whether she thought she could be happy in his palace. Beauty answered that everything was so beautiful and he was so kind that she would be very hard to please if she could not be happy here. Beauty began to think that the Beast was not nearly so terrible as she had

supposed at first. As he got up to leave her, he said in his gruff voice:

"I know I am only a Beast. Tell me, honestly, do you not think me very ugly?"

"Yes, Beast—since you wish the truth," said Beauty.

"Does my appearance horrify you?" he asked more gently.

And Beauty replied: "Not as much as it did at first. As you speak, and I see how kind you are, you begin to appear less ugly."

The Beast seemed pleased by her reply. He looked at her for a moment in silence. Then suddenly he said:

"Will you marry me?"

"Oh! What shall I say?" cried Beauty, for she was afraid to make the Beast angry by refusing.

"Say 'yes' or 'no' without fear," he replied.

"Oh, no, Beast!" said Beauty hastily.

"Good night, Beauty," he said. After he had left her she was very soon in bed and asleep, dreaming of her unknown prince. She thought he came and said to her:

"Ah, Beauty! How long will it take you to find me? How long, how long?"

And then her dreams changed, but the charming Prince figured in them all.

The days passed swiftly in different amusements. Every evening after supper the Beast came to see Beauty, and always before saying good night he would ask her in his terrible voice:

"Beauty, will you marry me?"

And it seemed to Beauty that now when she said "No, Beast," he went away quite sad.

One evening the Beast asked: "Does my visit to you every evening distress you?"

"Oh, no!" Beauty replied. "I look forward now to nine o'clock and if you did not come I should miss you very much. I have wanted many times to ask you why you do not sup with me."

The Beast shook his head sadly. "I do not wish to disgust you," he said, as he held up his paws. "You see, I am a beast—a monster."

To this Beauty replied tenderly, "There are many with the shape of men who have the heart of a monster. Better far to have the appearance of a monster and the heart of a man."

Now the Beast took a step toward her and said again:

"Beauty, will you marry me?"

Beauty was silent, for she hated to hurt him. At last she said gently, "No, Beast," and he left her in great distress.

So matters went on for many months, until at last, happy as she was, Beauty began to long for the sight of her father and sisters. One night, seeing her look very sad, the Beast asked her what troubled her. Beauty was no longer afraid of him, for she knew that he was really gentle in spite of his ferocious looks and his dreadful voice. So she answered that she was longing to see her home once more. Upon hearing this the Beast seemed sadly distressed, and cried miserably:

"Ah! Beauty, have you the heart to desert an unhappy Beast? What more do you want to make you happy? Is it because you hate me that you want to escape?"

"No, dear Beast," answered Beauty softly. "I do not hate you, and I should be very sorry never to see you any more. But I long to see my father again. Let me go for a week, and I promise to come back to you and stay for the rest of my life."

The Beast pleaded:

"I need you, Beauty. Without you I shall die."

Slowly Beauty repeated his words. "I have heard those words before," she said.

"They are true," said the Beast. "But I cannot refuse you anything you ask, even though it should cost me my life. Take the four boxes you will find in the room next to your own, and fill them with everything you wish to take with you. But remember your promise and come back when the week is over, for if you do not you will find your faithful Beast dead. You will not need any chariot to bring you back. Only say good-by to your father and sisters the night before you come away, and when you have gone to bed turn this ring around upon your finger and say firmly: 'I wish to go back to my palace and see my Beast again.'"

Then, taking a rose from a vase on the table, he said:

"Take this rose with you. It will remain fresh and alive for a week. Then it will begin to wilt. Its petals will fall and it will be dying. You will know then, if you do not return, that I too am dying.'' She saw that he was weeping.

"Good night, Beauty. Fear nothing, sleep peacefully, and before long you shall see your father once more.''

As soon as Beauty was alone she hastened to fill the boxes with all the rare and precious things she saw about her. Then she went to bed, and dreamed again of her beloved Prince.

A strange sound woke her—someone was speaking not very far away. Opening her eyes, she found herself in a room she had never seen before. Where could she be? She got up and dressed hastily, wondering by what magic the Beast had transported her to this strange place. Suddenly she heard her father's voice, and rushed out and greeted him joyfully. Her sisters were all astonished at her appearance, and there was no end to the questions they asked her. She had also much to hear about what had happened to them while she was away. But when they heard that she had come to be with them

only for a short time, and then must go back to the Beast's palace forever, they lamented loudly.

Then Beauty asked her father what he thought could be the

meaning of her strange dreams, and why the Prince constantly begged her not to trust to appearances. After much consideration he answered: "You tell me yourself that the Beast, frightful as he is, loves you dearly and deserves your love and gratitude for his gentleness and kindness. I think the Prince must mean that you ought to reward the Beast by doing as he wishes, in spite of his ugliness."

The time passed quickly, but Beauty often thought of the palace, of her dream Prince and of the kind and thoughtful Beast. She would not be sorry when the week was over and she would return to them. Her sisters seemed to have got quite used to being without her, and even found her rather in the way. But they had, nevertheless, been scheming together to keep her from going back, for they hoped that her failure to return would cause the Beast to die, and they might then take possession of his palace and his riches. "Why should *she* have more than we have?" they asked each other. So they persuaded their father to beg Beauty to stay a few days longer. Beauty found it hard to refuse him, for he seemed so unhappy at the thought of her leaving. "A few more days will do no harm," she told herself.

Then one night she had a dismal dream. She thought she heard groans which seemed to come from some bushes hiding the entrance of a cave, and running quickly to see what could be the matter, she found the Beast stretched out upon his side. He reproached her faintly with being the cause of his distress, and to her horror she saw that he was dying.

Beauty was terrified by this dream. When she awoke the next morning she suddenly saw that the rose at her bedside was wilting. Already some of the petals had fallen to the table. Hastily she got out of bed and reached for her ring on the table. It was not there. Her sisters had taken it while she slept, and were even now trying out its powers to see if it would work for their wishes. When they found that the ring only played tricks on them they fell to quarreling. Hearing this, Beauty hurried in to them. She picked up the precious ring which they had hastily thrown to the floor. Quickly she slipped the ring on her finger, turned it around as she had been told to do, and said:

"I wish to go back to the palace, and see my Beast again."

Instantly she was in the palace once more. Everything was just as before. But Beauty thought she had never known such a long day, for she was so anxious to see the Beast again that she felt as if supper-time would never come.

But when nine o'clock came and and no Beast appeared she was really frightened. So, after listening and waiting for a long time she ran down into the garden where she searched for him everywhere in vain. At last, quite tired, she saw that she was standing opposite the shady path she had seen in her dream. She rushed down it, and sure enough, there was the cave, and in it lay the Beast—asleep, as Beauty thought. She ran up and called to him, but to her horror he did not move or open his eyes.

"Oh! he is dead; and it is all my fault," said Beauty, crying bitterly. She threw herself down beside him and, taking one of his paws in her hand, stroked his head. He opened his eyes slowly.

"Oh! Beast, how you frightened me!" she cried. "I never knew how much I loved you until just now, when I feared I was too late to save your life."

"Can you really love such an ugly creature as I am?" said the Beast faintly. "Ah! Beauty, you came only just in time. I was dying because I thought you had forgotten your promise."

"No, dear Beast," said Beauty. "You shall not die. And I do not wish to live without you. I love you . . . and I want to marry you!"

As she spoke a blaze of light sprang up before the windows of the palace; fireworks crackled and guns banged, and across the avenue of orange trees, in letters all made of fireflies, was written: "Long live the Prince and his Bride!"

Turning to ask the Beast what it could all mean, Beauty found that he had disappeared; in his place stood the handsome Prince of the picture and her dream.

But Beauty cried, "Where is my Beast?"

"He is gone forever," said the Prince.

"No, no," said Beauty. "I want my Beast. I must go to find him."

"Wait, Beauty!" the Prince said. "Look at me. *I* was the Beast. A magician cast a spell over me and condemned me to remain in that form until a beautiful young woman should, of her own free will, consent to marry me. You, dear Beauty, have broken the spell."

"But why were you so punished?" Beauty asked.

"Because I was proud and thoughtless, vain and selfish, he made me look as I really was. But during the long years of my agony, I learned to know what it is to live unloved. And the pride and selfishness burned away until you were able to love me—even as the Beast."

"With all my heart," Beauty said. And they turned and went together into the beautifully lighted palace.

Their marriage was celebrated the very next day with the utmost splendor, and Beauty and the Prince lived happily ever after.

Rumpelstiltskin

Rumpelstiltskin

ILLUSTRATED BY LOUIS GLANZMAN

ONCE UPON A TIME THERE WAS a miller who was poor, but who was a great braggart. It happened one day that the miller had business with the King's Minister and, in order to seem important, he said, "I have a daughter who can spin straw in to gold."

The King's minister, who was a very greedy man, said to the miller, "That is an art which pleases me well! If your daughter is as clever as you say, bring her to the castle tomorrow, and I will put her to the test."

When the girl was brought to the King's Minister, he led her into a room which was all full of straw, gave her a spinning wheel and winder, and said, "Your father has told me of your great talent. Now set to work, and if by tomorrow morning you have not spun this straw into gold, I shall punish your father for telling such a lie."

There sat the poor miller's daughter, and for the life of her she did not know what to do. She had not the least idea how to spin straw into gold, and she became more and more worried, and at last she began to weep. All at once the door sprang open, and in stepped a tiny little man who said, "Good evening, miller's daughter, why are you weeping so?"

"Ah," answered the girl, "I have to spin straw into gold and I do not know how."

"Then," said the little man, "What will you give me if I spin it for you?"

"My necklace," said the maiden.

The little man took the necklace, seated himself at the spinning wheel, and *whir, whir, whir*—three times around and the reel was full. Then he put on another reel, and *whir, whir, whir*—three times around and the second reel also was full. So he went on till morning, when all the straw was spun and all the reels were full of gold.

At sunrise the King's Minister came, and when he saw the gold he was surprised and pleased, but he became all the more greedy for gold. He had the miller's daughter brought to another, much larger, room full of straw.

"If life is dear to you," he said, "you must spin all this straw into gold before morning."

The maiden did not know what to do and she began to weep. Then again the door sprang open and the little man appeared and said, "What will you give me if I spin the straw into gold?"

"The ring from my finger," answered the girl.

The little man took the ring, began to *whir* again at the spinning wheel, and by morning had spun all the straw into shining gold.

The King's Minister was delighted when he saw the masses of gold, but still he didn't have enough. He had the miller's daughter taken to a still larger room full of straw and said, "All this you must spin tonight. If you do not, you must die."

When the girl was alone, the little man came a third time and said, "What will you give me this time if I spin the straw for you?"

"I have nothing more that I can give," answered the girl.

"Then promise, if you become Queen, to give me your first child."

"What chance have I to become the Queen?" thought the maiden. "Surely it can do no harm to promise." So she agreed to do as the little man asked, and once more he spun the straw into gold.

When the King's Minister came in the morning and found everything as he had wished he let the girl go, for now he had all the gold he could ever use. But it happened that the King, who was young and handsome, saw the miller's daughter as she was leaving the castle through the garden, and fell in love with her.

He called his Minister and asked, "Who is that lovely maiden?"

"No one important," replied the Minister. "Just the miller's daughter who came here to deliver a bag of flour."

"Go fetch her at once and bring her here," the King commanded.

When the Minister brought the frightened maiden to the King, he spoke to her so kindly and his manner was so charming that she fell in love with him, too. And it was not long after that he brought the miller's daughter to the palace as his Queen.

A year later she brought a beautiful child into the world. She had forgotten all about the little man, when suddenly he entered her room and said, "Now give me what you promised."

The Queen was terrified and offered the little man all the riches of the kingdom if he would let her keep the child, but he said, "No, something living is dearer to me than all the treasures of the world."

Then the Queen began to weep so bitterly that the little man had pity on her and said, "I will give you three days, and if within that time you can find out my name, you shall keep your child."

All night long the Queen thought of every name she had ever heard, and she sent a messenger over the whole country to inquire what other names there were. When the little man came the next day, she began with Caspar, Melchior, Balzer, and named all the names she knew, one after the other; but each time the little man said, "That is not my name."

The second day she found out the names of all the people living near the castle. Then she repeated the strangest and most unusual names to the little man.

"Is your name perhaps Ribsteer or Sheepshanks or Stringbone?"

But each time he answered, "That is not my name."

The third day the messenger returned and said, "I haven't been able to find a single new name, but as I came to the corner of the wood on the side of a high mountain, where the fox and the hare bid each other good night, I saw a little house, and in front of the house a fire was burning, and around the fire the funniest little man was jumping and hopping on one leg and crying out:

> *"Tonight I brew, tomorrow I bake,*
> *And then the child away I'll take;*
> *For little knows the Royal Dame*
> *That* RUMPELSTILTSKIN *is my name."*

You can imagine how happy the Queen was when she heard the name. Soon after that the little man came again and asked, "Well, Your Majesty, what is my name?"

The Queen asked, "Is your name Cornelius?"

"No."

"Is it Frederick?"

"No."

"Are you perhaps called Rumpelstiltskin?"

"A witch has told you that—a witch has told you that!" shrieked the little man, and he fled to the woods in a rage and was never seen again.

The Sleeping Beauty

The Sleeping Beauty

ILLUSTRATED BY GRACE CLARKE

ONCE UPON A TIME in a kingdom not too near and not too far, there lived a King and Queen who had everything in the world they wanted, except the one thing they wished for most. They had no children, and they longed to have a son or a daughter.

One day, as the Queen was sitting by the side of the lake lost in sad thoughts, a tiny fairy rose up from the water and gave her a white flower. "Take this," said the fairy, "and your dearest wish will be fulfilled."

The Queen was overjoyed when at last a beautiful baby daughter was born to her. The King was so delighted that he ordered a great christening feast be held, the like of which had never been seen before.

Messengers were sent out to invite all the fairies in the kingdom to be godmothers to the Princess. Six good fairies were found, and they all came to honor the royal baby.

The christening took place with great pomp and splendor. After the christening the guests returned to the castle for the royal banquet. Before each fairy was placed a plate, knife, and spoon of pure gold. But just as they were about to sit down at the banquet table an unexpected guest appeared, her untidy clothes all rusty black. She was an old and ugly fairy who had not been invited because the messengers had not known where to find her. The King ordered another place to be set for her, but as he had no more golden dishes and spoons, hers had to be ordinary ones. At this she became very angry, feeling that she was not being as well treated as the others, and one of the younger fairies heard her muttering angry threats. When the banquet was over, the young fairy, fearing that the Black Fairy would try to harm the Princess, hid herself behind the curtains to be ready to help if need be.

Now each of the fairies came forward to present their gifts to the Princess. Being fairies, their gifts of good wishes were sure to come true. The first fairy said, "My gift to the Princess is that she shall become the most beautiful woman in the world." The second said, "She shall be as good as she is beautiful." The third said, "She shall be graceful in everything she does." The fourth said, "She shall dance like a leaf on a summer breeze." The fifth said, "She shall sing like the nightingale."

Then came the turn of the Black Fairy. Spitefully she said,

> "Before the child is woman grown
> She shall reap what you have sown!
> The spell is wound, the deed is planned—
> A spindle-point shall pierce her hand.
> All shall cease, and she will lie
> Deep in sleep until she die."

The King and Queen were almost beside themselves with grief.
But now the young fairy who had hidden behind the curtains
flew to the side of the Princess's cradle, and said:

"O King and Queen, do not weep! I cannot entirely undo the
evil wished by the old fairy, but the Princess shall not die. For here is
my gift to her:

> *"Safe from passion, safe from strife*
> *Safe from all that threatens life*
> *None shall touch her, naught shall shake her*
> *Till a true Prince comes to wake her."*

Now the King did everything in his power to prevent the misfortune foretold by the Black Fairy. He commanded that no one in
the whole kingdom, on pain of death, should spin with a spindle. All
the spinning wheels in the kingdom were to be burned.

In time the little Princess grew into a beautiful young girl, and
all the good wishes of the fairies came true. Great care was taken
that she should never know of such a thing as a spinning wheel.

One evening when she was just fifteen years old she was alone
in her room, preparing to go to bed. Suddenly she thought she heard
a strange whirring sound. Opening her door, she followed the sound
which seemed to come from far above her. After climbing many
stairs, she came to the top of a tall tower. A door opened into a small

room she had never seen before. In it sat a very old woman — busy at her spinning wheel.

"Come in, child," said the old woman, beckoning.

"What are you doing, Granny?" asked the Princess.

"I'm spinning, my pretty child," said the woman.

For a moment the Princess watched, fascinated. Then she said: "Let me see if I can do it."

As she said this she picked up the spindle, and then—the point of the spindle pierced her finger. At once she fell into a deep sleep.

At this same moment everything ceased to move in the palace and everyone fell asleep. The King and Queen, dressing in their rooms, fell asleep at once, and with them the courtiers, the pages, the footmen, and all the servants. The cook, who was just about to box the kitchen boy's ears because he had made a mistake, fell asleep, and the boy did too. The horses went to sleep in the stable, the cock in the yard, the doves on the roof, and the flies on the wall.

All around the castle, there now grew up a hedge of briars and thorns so tough and thick that it seemed as if no one could ever get through it. Nothing could be seen of the castle but the high tower where the lovely Princess slept.

From time to time princes in far countries heard of the Sleeping Beauty. The story was told by fathers to sons, and by sons to their sons. Many tried to reach the castle, but none could get through the thorny hedge, and many perished in the wild jungle that had grown up there.

At last just a hundred years had passed. On that very day a king's son came riding through the land, and when he heard the story of the Sleeping Beauty, he vowed that he would awaken her. As he came to the thorny hedge, the branches gave way and let him pass. The gates, overgrown with briars, swung open as he approached. When he entered the courtyard, what a sight met his eyes! The cock was asleep, and so were the horses in their stalls, and the doves that perched, with heads under their wings, on the roof. In the kitchen the cook was asleep, with his hand raised as if to strike the sleeping kitchen boy beside him. All the guards about the castle slept quietly, and in the royal chambers the King and Queen and all the ladies and gentlemen of the court were asleep, caught in the very posture of what they were doing so long ago.

At last the Prince reached the tower where the Princess slept. Eagerly he opened the door of the little room. There lay the Princess, as fresh and lovely as on the day she fell asleep. The Prince bent down and gently kissed her. She opened her eyes and smiled. "Is it you, Prince?" she murmured; "I have waited for you a long time."

And now the whole castle awoke. The King and Queen and all their attendants rubbed their eyes and looked about them. The horses in the stable got up and shook themselves. The cock began to crow. The doves on the roof lifted their heads from under their wings and began to coo. The royal standard on its pole waved in the breeze. The flies on the wall began to crawl again. In the kitchen the cook boxed the boy's ears so hard that he cried out. The fire on the hearth blazed up, and the meat went on roasting.

Hand in hand the Prince and Princess went down the tower stairs. Very soon their wedding was celebrated with all splendor, and they lived long and happily together.

Other titles in this series

Published by

RANDOM HOUSE, INC., 457 Madison Avenue, New York 22, N. Y.

IF YOU ENJOYED READING THE STORIES IN THIS book, you will want to have the *complete,* beautifully illustrated edition of SHIRLEY TEMPLE'S STORYBOOK which contains the following stories:

BEAUTY AND THE BEAST

THE VALIANT LITTLE TAILOR

RAPUNZEL

THE MAGIC FISHBONE

THE NIGHTINGALE

RUMPELSTILTSKIN

DICK WHITTINGTON AND HIS CAT

RIP VAN WINKLE

THE SLEEPING BEAUTY

THE LITTLE LAME PRINCE

ALI BABA AND THE FORTY THIEVES

THE LAND OF GREEN GINGER

THE EMPEROR'S NEW CLOTHES

THE LEGEND OF SLEEPY HOLLOW

THE WILD SWANS

Fifteen of the best-known artists in America were selected to illustrate SHIRLEY TEMPLE'S STORYBOOK. Their enchanting drawings, along with stories that have stood the test of time, make this book a treasured possession for any child.

RANDOM HOUSE, NEW YORK